This Topsy and Tim book belongs to

_____

Topsy and Tim
Have Itchy Heads

By Jean and Gareth Adamson

Illustrations by Belinda Worsley

A catalogue record for this book is available from the British Library

Published by Ladybird Books Ltd
A Penguin Company
Penguin Books Ltd., 80 Strand, London WC2R 0RL, UK
Penguin Books Australia Ltd., 707 Collins Street, Melbourne, Victoria 3008, Australia
Penguin Group (NZ) 67 Apollo Drive, Rosedale, North Shore 0632, New Zealand

002

ISBN: 978-1-40930-720-4
Printed in China

www.topsyandtim.com

Topsy and Tim had itchy heads, but nobody noticed them scratching. Mummy didn't notice and Dad didn't notice.

Then, one Friday afternoon, Topsy and Tim came running out of school with a letter for Mummy and Dad. All the other children had letters, too. The letter said: "Dear Parents, There is an outbreak of head lice at school. Please check your child's hair. The enclosed leaflet will explain what to look for."

Mummy showed the letter to Dad.

"Topsy and Tim can't possibly have head lice," said Mummy.

"We often shampoo their hair."

"Head lice love clean hair," said Topsy. "Miss Terry said so."

Facts about head lice

What do they look like?

- Very small, semi-transparent and brown.

- Louse eggs and nits [empty egg shells] are found glued to hairs, near the roots.

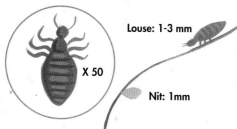

Louse: 1-3 mm

X 50

Nit: 1mm

- Headlice can be difficult to spot.

- They don't always cause itching.

- Often, there are only a few on the head.

- Wash, rinse, condition and use the special comb to find them.

How do they spread?

- They clamber from head to head.

- They do not hop, jump or live in hats.

Dad read the leaflet carefully. It said all sorts of interesting things about head lice.

"It makes me feel itchy to think about it," said Dad, scratching his head.

That night, at bath time, Mummy had a good look in Topsy's hair – and she couldn't believe what she found.

"Come quickly!" she yelled to Dad.

Dad came running to see what was wrong.

"Topsy has got nits!" said Mummy.

"Have I got nits?" asked Tim.

Dad looked in Tim's hair.

"Tim's got nits too," he said.

It was too late to do anything about it that night, but early the next morning Dad hurried to the chemist's. "We need something to get rid of head lice," he said. "Try this bottle of special lotion. I've sold a lot lately," said the chemist.

As soon as Dad got home, Mummy rubbed the lotion on to Topsy's hair and Dad did Tim's. They had to be careful not to get it in their eyes.

Then Topsy and Tim played in the garden and let the breeze dry their hair. Both of them were glad when it was time to wash the lotion off.

On Sunday, Louise Lewis came to play with Topsy and Tim. Mummy saw them with their heads close together.

"Oh dear," she thought. "If Louise has got head lice, Topsy and Tim could catch them again."

On Monday morning, on the way to school,
Topsy and Tim met Tony Welch.
"We had nits in our hair," said Topsy.
"I've had nits three times," said Tony.

Josie Miller helped Topsy and Tim hang their coats
up in the cloakroom.
"We had head lice lotion on our hair," Tim told her.
"It smelled awful."
"I don't use that lotion because I've got asthma,"
said Josie.

Topsy and Tim told Miss Terry about their nits and the
head lice lotion.

"I'm glad you got rid of those naughty creepy crawlies,"
said Miss Terry. "I've got some nice little mini-beasts for
you to look at today."

The nice mini-beasts were all in jam jars on Miss Terry's table. There were ladybirds, woodlice, snails and caterpillars. The children looked at them with magnifying glasses. It was very interesting.

When Tim was tired of looking at the mini-beasts he
looked at Topsy's head with his magnifying glass.
"I can see a mini-beast on Topsy's hair!" he said.
Miss Terry came to look.
"Oh dear, Topsy," she said. "I'm afraid it's a head louse."

At home time Miss Terry told Mummy about the head louse on Topsy's hair. Mummy was very upset and Topsy began to cry.

"What's wrong with Topsy?" asked Kerry.
"Topsy's got head lice again and she hates the smelly lotion," said Tim.
"You don't have to use that lotion to get rid of them," said Kerry's mum. "Come home with us and we'll show you what we do."

Soon they were all squeezed into Kerry's bathroom.
Mummy and Tim and Kerry sat in a row on the edge
of the bath and watched what Kerry's mum did.
First she washed Topsy's hair with ordinary shampoo
and then she squirted lots of conditioner on it.

Next Kerry's mum combed Topsy's hair, while it was still wet, with a special little fine-toothed comb. "I'm combing Topsy's hair from the roots, very carefully, all over," said Kerry's mum.

She combed three little lice out and kept on combing but there were no more. Kerry's mum washed and combed Tim's and Kerry's hair too, just in case.
There were no creepy crawlies in Tim's or Kerry's hair.

Mummy helped Topsy and Tim and Kerry to dry
their hair.
"This is like being at the hairdressers," said Topsy.
"Come and have some lemonade and biscuits,"
called Kerry's mum from the kitchen.

"I need to get a special comb like Kerry's for Topsy," said Mummy. "If I check her hair with the fine-toothed comb while it's wet, I will catch any baby lice as they hatch."

"You look very happy," said Dad when they got back home.
"We are," said Topsy. "We've found a good way to get rid
of naughty nits."
"No more itchy heads!" said Tim.
"Let's hope so!" said Dad.

*Now turn the page and help
Topsy and Tim solve a puzzle.*

Look at the two pictures of Topsy and Tim with itchy heads.
There are six tricky differences between the pictures.
Can you spot them all?

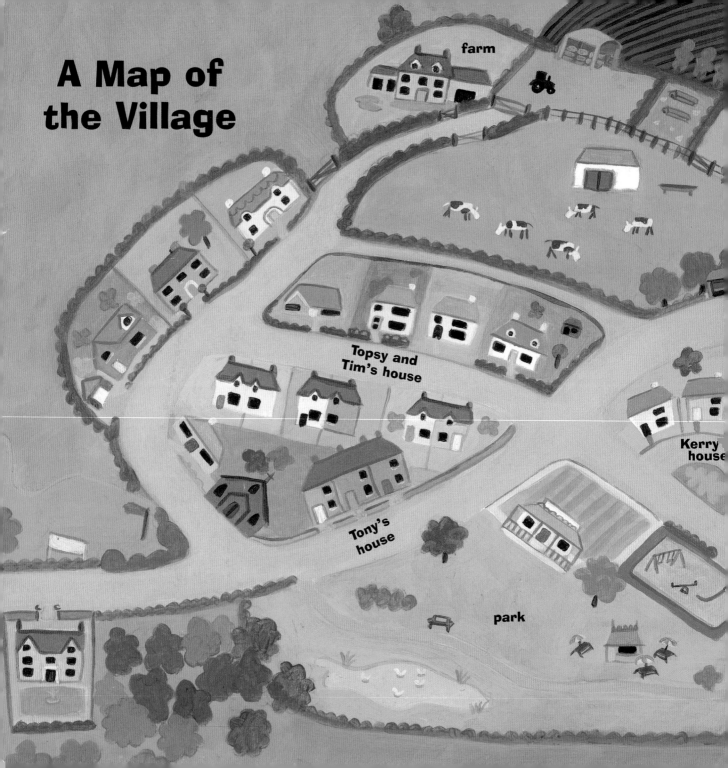

A Map of the Village

farm

Topsy and
Tim's house

Tony's
house

Kerry
house

park

garage

health centre

post office

church

primary school

nursery school

police station

Have you read all the Topsy and Tim stories?

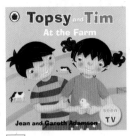
At the Farm
9781409303367

Go Camping
9781409303336

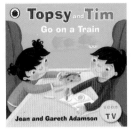
Go on an Aeroplane
9781409300571

Go on a Train
9781409304241

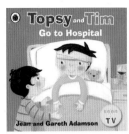
Go to Hospital
9781409304234

Start School
9781409300830

Go to the Doctor
9781409303343

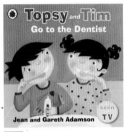
Go to the Dentist
9781409300588

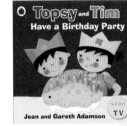
Have a Birthday Party
9781409300618

Meet Father Christmas
9781409311591

Meet the Police
9781409308836

Go to the Zoo
9781409300847

Meet the Firefighters
9781409307211

Learn to Swim
9781409300601

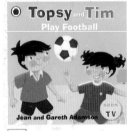
Play Football
9781409303350

Safety First
9781409308829

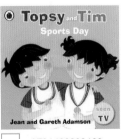
Sports Day
9781409309468

Have Itchy Heads
✓ 9781409307204

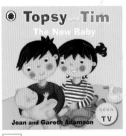
The New Baby
9781409300564

Visit London
9781409309475

Available on the App Store

The Topsy and Tim app is available for iPad, iPhone and iPod touch.

It is also available on Android devices.